H & F

D1033527

from

TAAMIR

&

HANIYA

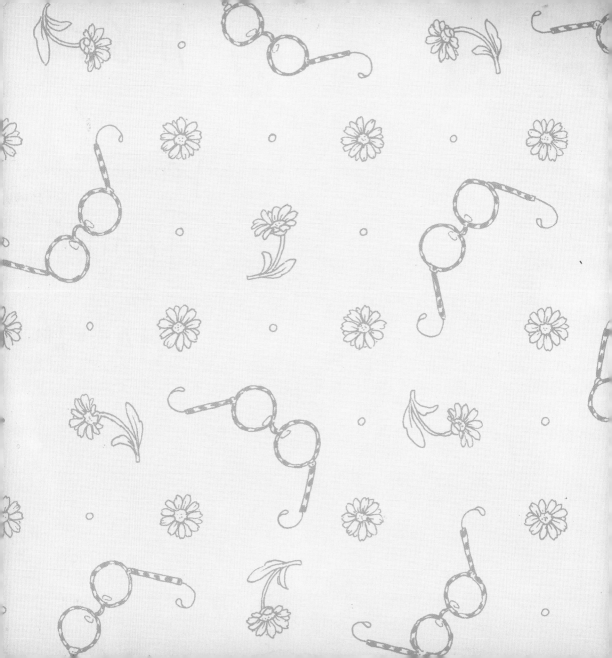

Daisy & Jack

IN THE GARDEN

For Lucy

Daisy & Jack
IN THE GARDEN

Prue Theobalds

Uplands Books

One day Jack and Daisy decided
to make a garden.

"You make your garden here,"
said Jack, "and I will make mine on
the other side of the shed".

Jack took a spade and began to dig.

"Daisy, what will you grow in
your garden?" he asked.

"I don't know. I'm thinking,"

said Daisy.

Jack planted a row of carrot seeds,
a row of lettuce seeds
and some beans.

"Daisy, what are you planting in your garden?" he asked.

"I'm still thinking," said Daisy.

Jack and Daisy spent every day in their gardens. Sometimes it rained.

Sometimes the sun shone.

Jack's vegetables were growing fast.

But Daisy said her garden
was a secret.

Every day Jack's vegetables looked bigger. "Is your garden growing?" he asked Daisy.

But Daisy did not answer.

Jack picked some of his vegetables
to show Daisy.
"I am coming to see what you
have grown." he said.

"Just flowers!" said Daisy.

First Published 1997 by Uplands Books
1 The Uplands, Maze Hill, St Leonards-on-Sea,
East Sussex, TN38 0HL, England

ISBN 1 897951 15 9

Text and illustrations © *Prue Theobalds 1997*
The moral right of the Author/illustrator has been asserted

Printed in Singapore

British Library
Cataloguing-in-Publication Data
A catalogue record for this book is available
from the British Library

also in this series

Daisy & Jack and the Surprise Pie

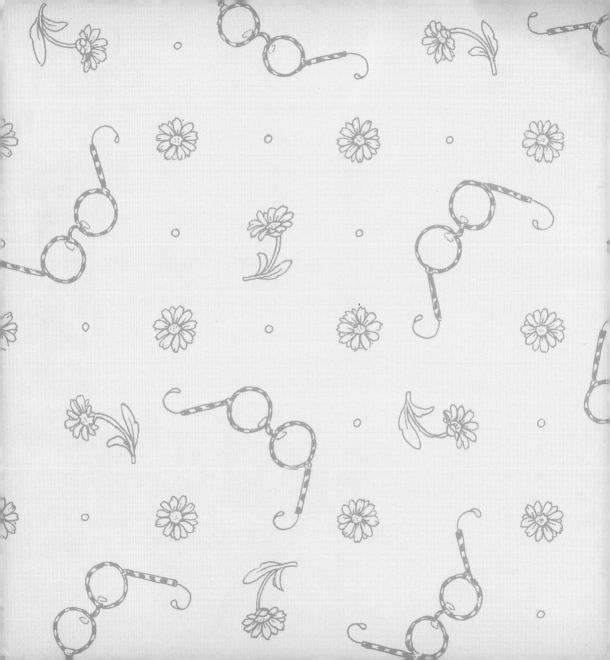